The
Last Acts
of Saint
Fuck You

by Bern Porter

THE
LAST ACTS
OF SAINT
FUCK YOU

collages by Steve Perkins

2008
Xexoxial Editions
West Lima, Wisconsin

Originally published by Xerox Sutra Editions 1985.
Book & cover designed by mIEKAL aND.
Photographs of Bern Porter by Amy Hufnagel.
3rd edition 2008.

ISBN-13 978-0-9770049-6-6
ISBN-10 0-9770049-6-1

published by

Xexoxial Editions
10375 Cty Hway Alphabet
La Farge, WI 54639

perspicacity@xexoxial.org
www.xexoxial.org

The anxiety image-bank, or some thoughts about Bern Porter before I eat lunch

He does not live in a mail box as I had once thought. Can one acquire virtuosity to FINDING the exact peculiar pieces of information as to reveal unheard of notions & would it all fit into a scheme in some one man's head in faraway Maine? Has as Bern Porter's books suggest, an eclectic anarchy changed the course of pages of paper between covers? In a generation with video display instant access information & other forms of hypodermic information processing, can the needs, desires, & wants of books be drastically rerouted so as to include previously unhad ideas & images? Is it that Bern Porter has constructed with his books an universal epic of signs passing before our eyes daily, or how you say? Everything is passing for something else until we know what were seeing.

~mIEKAL aND

The abnegating of treaties
The acidifying of alkalis
The affiliating of bastards
The aligning of booby-traps
The ambulating of cripples
The annuling of covenants
The assessing of polls

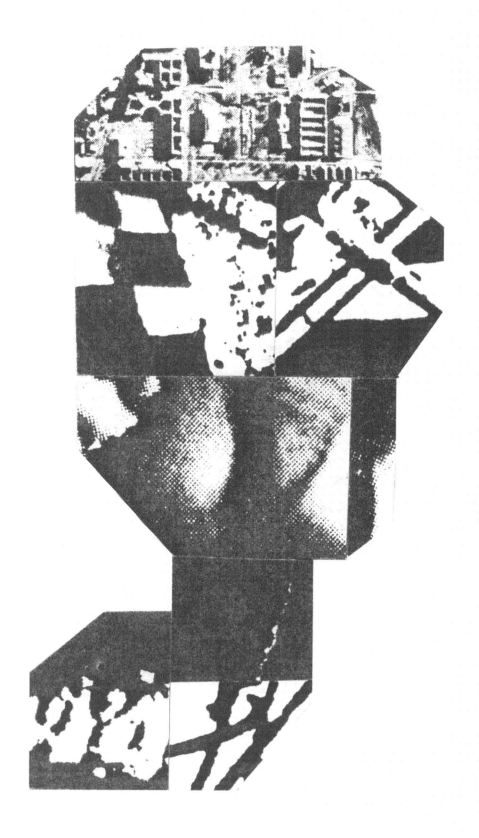

b

The baiting of suckers
The banishing of believers
The beating of bare-asses
The bilking of swindlers
The breeding of monsters
The brining of sweets
The bursting of influence

C

The camouflaging of enemies
The castrating of males
The causing of disasters
The certifying of devils
The clogging of conduits
The coloring of statistics
The cross-breeding of delinquents

d

The declaring of treason
The deducting of nonallowables
The deflowering of virgins
The defoliating of positions
The depreciating of standards
The dispensing of allergies
The distorting of basics

e

The edifying of traitors
The effacing of documents
The elapsing of contracts
The elevating of expectations
The enjoining of opposites
The extolling of crime
The exuding of stenches

The fermenting of riots
The firing of bins
The flouting of justice
The flunking of brilliants
The foreclosing of mortgages
The foreshortening of hymens
The framing of innocent

g

The gassing of stalwarts
The getting of bribes
The goading of downtroddens
The gowning of nudes
The grabbing of succulents
The grading of dropouts
The griming of runways

The hacking of corpses
The halving of totals
The harassing of taxpayers
The heeding of irrelevancies
The higgling of principles
The hosing of affluents
The humiliating of officials

i

The idling of servants
The igniting of fires
The immolating of nuns
The impeaching of innocents
The implying of gloom
The improvising of traps
The imputing of sins

The jabbering of smut
The jacobinizing of Baptists
The jamming of frequencies
The jaundicing of springs
The jibbing of progress
The jobbing of pot
The jockeying of funds

The kecking of wines
The keelhauling of delinquents
The kenning of gossip
The kicking of publicans
The killing of civilians
The kindling of rages
The kiting of bills

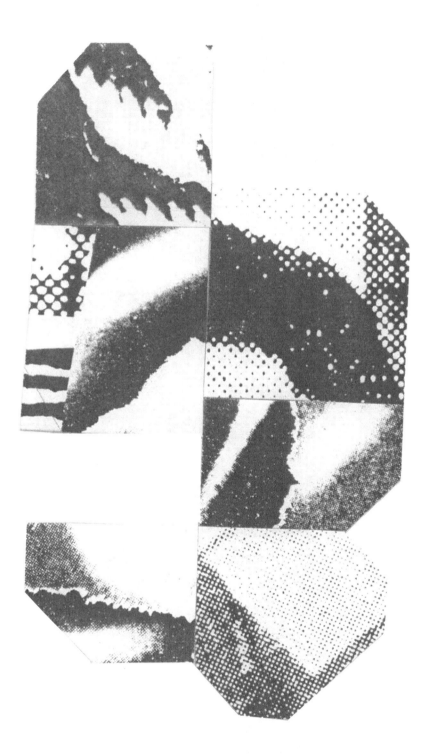

1

The lacerating of boils
The lacqueying of sleepwalkers
The lading of backs
The lamming of widows
The lapidating of humans
The laying of pits
The liberating of demons

The machinating of designs
The mazing of clarity
The menacing of enfants
The metastising of tumors
The milking of treasuries
The minimizing of importants
The multiplying of venom

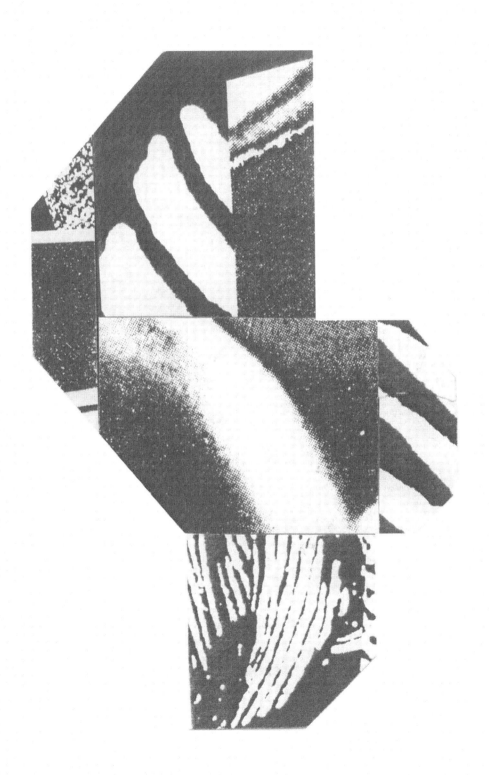

The naming of misers
The napping of covers
The narrating of contradictions
The naturalizing of criminals
The nidificating of vats
The non-processing of plaintiffs
The non-plusing of laities

The obfuscating of patrons
The obligating of commoners
The obsessing of jealots
The obtunding of blades
The occuring of misfortunes
The originating grievances
The overriding of objections

The padding of claims
The palliating of excesses
The pandering of lusts
The paralyzing of arteries
The poaching of game
The polluting of drains
The purveying of deceptions

The queering of sexes
The quelling of righteousness
The querrying of innocents
The quibbling of facts
The quintupling of births
The quitting of scenes
The quoting of doom

The rabbling of mobs
The radiating of hate
The raffling of studs
The rankling of wounds
The raping of Europa
The recognizing of lesbians
The reselling of contraceptives

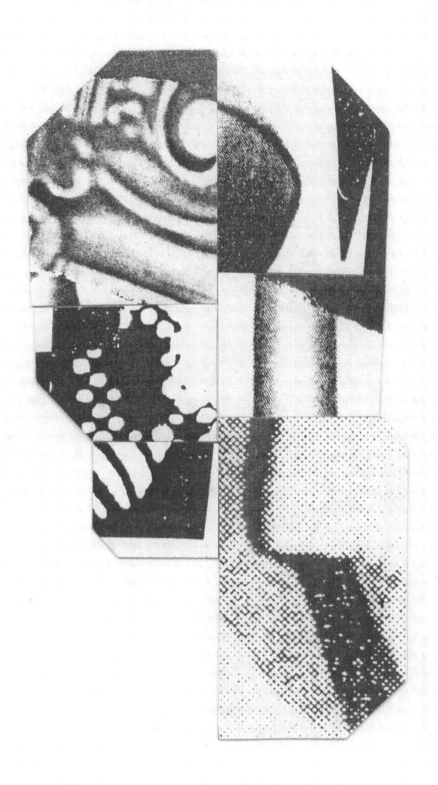

S

The salting of sores
The sacking of altars
The sanctifying of evils
The scaffolding of baptistries
The shattering of nerves
The shifting of blame
The snatching of lightbulbs

The tabulating of theiveries
The teaching of adultery
The tempting of losers
The terrifying of dreamers
The tightening of girdles
The tinging of heirlooms
The twisting of arms

The ulcerating of pimples
The ululating of laments
The unbarring of vaults
The unbuckling of stays
The underplaying of supplicants
The unfrocking of bishops
The unleashing of serpents

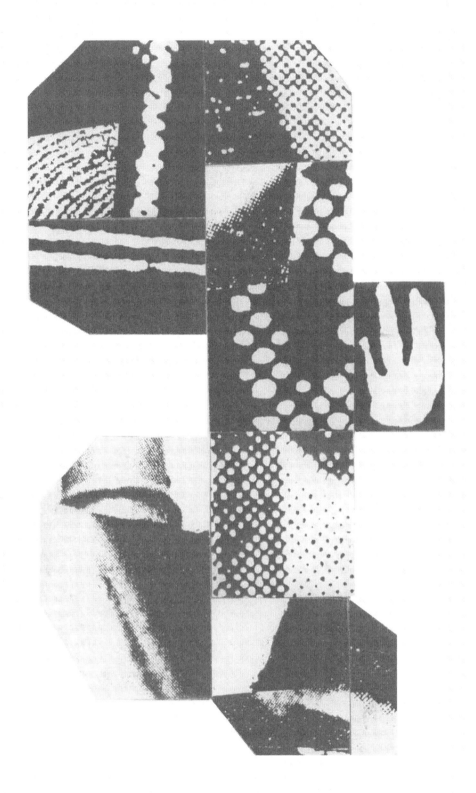

The vacating of leases
The validating of forgeries
The vanquishing of warriors
The varnishing of reality
The vaunting of lies
The vouching of makeshifts
The vulgarizing of priests

The wading of reservoirs
The waging of revolutions
The waiving of vetos
The warding of peacelovers
The weighing of doubts
The wrecking of matches
The wringing of debts

The xerographing of copyrights
The xeroxing of xeroxes
The x-ing of entries
The x-radiating of negatives
The xylographing of obscenities
The xylophoning of dirges
The xystering of skulls

The yammering of joys
The yapping of gossip
The yarding of parishioners
The yielding of victories
The yoking of unequals
The yowling of greetings
The yuling of Easter

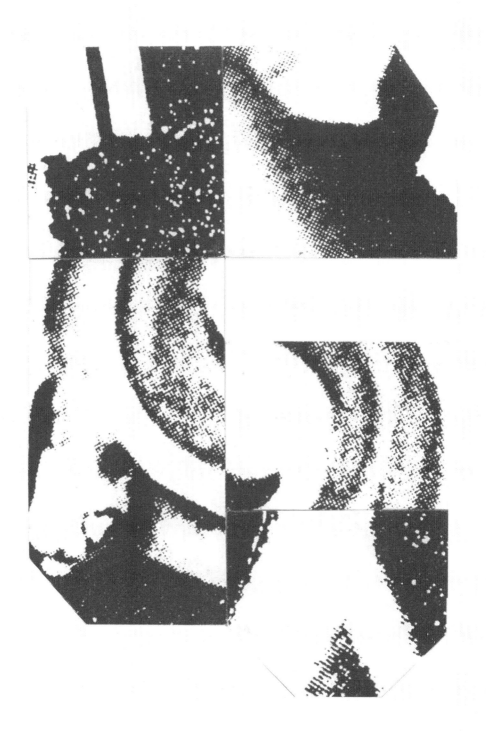

Z

The zeroing of gains
The zesting of misery
The zinging of drums
The zipping of stays
The zooming of dirigibles
The zoning of beaches
The zounding of oaths

THE LAST ACTS
OF SAINT FUCK
YOU
THE LAST
ACTS OF SAINT
FUCK YOU
ACTS OF
SAINT FUCK
YOU THE LAST
ACTS OF
SAINT FUCKYOU

Steve Perkins photo by Bill Washburn

Bern Porter TITLES published by Xexoxial

MY MY DEAR ME
1985, 7x8.5, 20 pgs. Our first Porter book is a sampler of minimally manipulated found material. Visual dichotomies as seen from a speeding getaway car. If you don't know about Bern Porter, go find out.

THE LAST ACTS OF SAINT FUCK YOU
1985, 2008. 5.5x8.5, 44 pgs. With collages by Steve Perkins (Box of Water). This is probably the only writing we've seen by Bern Porter. An alphabet book   which in 40-some pages sums up the world vision of the disinherited. Bern is the Director of the Institute for Advanced Thinking in Belfast, Maine. [Bern renders this work, in two different audio versions, on "Williamson Street Blues" - See Audio Muzixa Qet section of this catalogue]

WHY MY LEFT LEG IS HOT
1988, 8.5x11, 64 pgs, color. For the Bern Porter collector, special color edition of his video of the same name. For over 40 years Bern has been collecting bits of this & that. This book is an epic of legs, a vocabulary of limbs, & an un-doing of pornography.

CRCNCL / a sur surrealistic SCRIPT.
1990, 8.5x11, 40 pages, $5. Xerox of holograph edition of the film script of movie of the same name.

XEROLAGE 16
1990, 8.5x11, 24 pgs. That crazy man from Maine came & visited us again. He has been dying to do a Xerolage so I took him to the copy shop. He had spied a couple images from Michael VooDoo that he wanted to work with & the whole issue stems from manipulating xerox treatments of them.

WUONDRUSHK
2004, 72 pages, 8.5x11, color. Version 1.0. founds, collages, correspondence & ephemera from Bern's residency @ the Church of Anarchy (Madison, WI). "I wasn't expecting to find another Bern Porter manuscript in the bottom of a box in the closet. It's funny what you can tell about a man by the pages he cuts out of magazines or finds in someone's trash when they're not looking. Find in Bern what Bern found in it." ~mIEKAL aND.

PDF book download: high resolution file suitable for printing (300dpi, 13.3mb) (printing hint: pages 1 + 74 are the covers. print pages 2-73 back to back)
http://xexoxial.org/is/wuondrushk/by/bern_porter

HOLD ONTO YOUR HAT: BERN PORTER INTERVIEWS AND MISCELLANEA
2008, forthcoming. Unpublished interviews, photographs, miscellanea relating
to Porter's Institute of Advanced Thinking. Interviews by Judith Hoffberg, Dick
Higgins, mIEKAL aND, Elizabeth Was, Ben Meyers, Andrew Russ, phobrek hei
& others. Photographs by Amy Huffnagel & Read Brugger.

SOUND

WILLIAMSON STREET BLUES
1988, 60 minutes. Bern renders two versions of his "Last Acts of St. Fuck
You", reads Chinese poetry, improvises an epic performance of the Madison
phonebook, & more.

WILLIAMSON STREET NIGHT
1989, 60 minutes. Recorded during Bern's Dec 1989 Madison
materialization. Side One is Bern reading from Abraham Lincoln Gillespie &
Malok talking off the cuff. Also on this side is Bern reading from Abraham
Lincoln Gillespie & Miekal And reading from his own book Raw. Sway. Aloud.
simultaneously accompanied by a recording of the Wakanaki Indians. Side
Two is Bern reading from Abraham Lincoln Gillespie & Liz Was reading Rooms
by Gertude Stein. Note that all "reading" were renderings & not word-for-word.

ASPECTS OF MODERN POETRY
1990, 35 minutes. Recorded live on WBAI, NYC sometime in 1982 with
Robert Holman. Bern talking about the true essence of the word & where it
could go.

FOUND SOUNDS
1990, 60 minutes. Side One is Bern in session with Dick Higgins & Charlie
Morrow recorded Dec 2, 1978. Side Two is Bern in concert with Patricia
Burgess, tenor sax; Charlie Morrow, brass, ocarinas, voice; Glen Velez,
bodhran, tambourine, cymbals; recorded on May 9, 1981. Originally produced
by New Wilderness Audiographics but no longer available.

THE ETERNAL POETRY FESTIVAL
1990, 60 minutes. A stream-of-consciousness sound poetry improvisation
with fellow Maine publisher/writer Mark Melnicove. Date of recording is vague,
perhaps sometime in 1979. "for our friends in Germany."

VIDEO

CRCNCL / A SUR-SURREALISTIC
1995, 60 minutes. A video movie starring Bern Porter & 2 year old Liaizon Wakest with words by Abraham Lincoln Gillespie. Created during Bern's Dec 1989 Madison materialization. This is a gestalt of visual poetry, performance poetry, spanning nearly a century of accumulated experiences. Camera as found observer, performer as a new species of language. Videographers were Gregib M & Steve Rife.

WHY MY LEFT LEG IS HOT
1988, 89 minutes. This "bookideo" features found eroticism from the master of collecting the unwanted. Color video of more than 200 collages with discrete body sounds by E. Was. A delirium of legs in the hot of the night. Audio visual wallpaper for the literate future.

WHY MY LEFT LEG IS HOT (remix)
2005, 1 minute re-edit of 225 erotic Porter founds. re-edit by Camille Bacos, audio by mIEKAL aND, and jUStin katKO.

Bern Porter TITLES published by other publishers

Mark Melnicove and Bern Porter
The Eternal Poetry Festival
216 Cedar Grove Road
Dresden, ME 04342
mmelnicove@roadrunner.com

Bern (Poster)
Bern Porter International, 1975. 17.5 x 22.5 inches.
Visual Founds iconic autobiography.

The Book of Do's
Dog Ear Press, 1982, 0-937966-11-8, 8.5 x 11 inches, 400 pages.
Visual Founds—Do this, do that, etc.

The First Publications of F. Scott Fitzgerald.
Walton Press (Bern Porter International). 5.5 x 8.5 inches. 12 pages.
Bibliography of Fitzgerald's writings as initially published.

Gee-Whizzels
Bern Porter International, 1975. 8.5 x 11 inches. 72 pages.
Visual Founds that come at us like pieces chipped off of the Tower of Babel.

Here Comes Everybody's Don't Book
Dog Ear Press, 1984, 0-937966-15-0, 8.5 x 11 inches, 400 pages.
Visual Founds–Don't do this, don't do that, etc.

H.L. Mencken: A Bibliography
Bern Porter International, 1965 edition. 5.5 x 11 inches. 24 pages.
Just what it says it is

The Last Acts of Saint Fuck You (poster)
Bern Porter International, 1975. 17.5 x 22.5 inches.
Perhaps the greatest poem ever, printed in its entirety on a single sheet in
non-serif type.

The Manhattan Phone Book.
Abyss Publications, 1972. 5.5 x 8.5 inches. 300 pages.
Visual Founds—Alphabet book cut out from actual NYC phone book.

Monica Lewinsky All of Us Want Yours
Roger Jackson, Publisher, 1998. 4.25 x 11 inches. 16 pages.
8-part poem with 2-dimensional cigar inserted.

OKRAZOIDICAL II (with John A. Pyros)
Dramatika, 1996. 8.5 x 11 inches. 42 pages.
Collaborative assembling of Bern's founds and Pryos' writings.

See(MAN)TIC
Light Work, 1994. 9 x 7.5 inches. 36 pages.
Catalogue of Porter's founds and writings from show at Robert B. Menschel
Photography Gallery, Syracuse, NY.

Sounds That Arouse Me
Tilbury House, Publishers, 1992. 0-88448-101-8. 5.5 x 8.5 inches. 172
pages.
Edited and with an introduction by Mark Melnicove. "Best of" prose, poetry,
founds from 1940s to 1992.

Sweet End
Dog Ear Press, 1989, 8.5 x 11 inches, 400 pages.
Visual Founds all about death and dying.

13/17
Backwoods Broadsides, Number 11. 1995. 8.5 x 14 inches.
Found photo sequence in one-page "chaplet" format.

The Wastermaker, 1926-1961.
Abyss Publications, 1972. 5.5 x 8.5 inches, 300 pages.
Visual Founds—The groundbreaking masterpiece.

What Henry Miller Said and Why It is So Important (Poster)
Bern Porter International, 1975. 17.5 x 22.5 inches.
The classic prose-poem statement by Porter on Miller's work. Illustrated by
Opal Nations.

Where to Go, What to Do, When You Are Bern Porter
Tilbury House, Publishers, 1992. 0-88448-125-5 (cloth). 0-88448-126-3
(paper). 5.5 x 8.5 inches. 348 pages.
Biography of Bern Porter by Porter's long-time poet-playwright-friend, James
Schevill. Generously illustrated with photographs of and visual founds by
Porter.

Where to Go, What to Do, When You Are in New York, Week of June 17, 1972
Bern Porter International, 1975, 8.5 x 11 inches. 72 pages.
Visual Founds alteration of weekly entertainment guide, meant to strangle the reader.

Bern Porter TITLES published by Runaway Spoon Press

Box 495597, Port Charlotte FL 33949
http://comprepoetica.com/RASP/RASP.html

Neverends
    Introduction by Erika Pfander
    A collage sequence whose subject is existence, from lightning through shoe advertisements to flowers in bloom
    The Runaway Spoon Press. 50 pages, 4.25" by 5.5". Publication Date: 16 April 1988. ISBN 0-926935-03-8.

Numbers
    Introduction by Erika Pfander
    A waggish collage sequence concerned with the varied ways numbers take part in everyday life
 The Runaway Spoon Press. 52 pages, 4.25" by 5.5". Publication Date: 29 July 1989. ISBN 0-926935-20-8.

Signs
    Introduction by Erika Pfander
    The final volume of Porter's four-volume investigation of human communication
 The Runaway Spoon Press. 46 pages, 4.25" by 5.5". Publication Date: 31 December 1996. ISBN 1-57141-025-2.

Symbols
    Simple-seeming but eye-opening collages by the master
 The Runaway Spoon Press. 42 pages, 4.25" by 5.5". Publication Date: 28 June 1995. ISBN 0-57141-015-5.

Vocrascends (with Malok)
    A satirical/lyrical high-art/crude collage sequence by two legends of the mail art scene
 The Runaway Spoon Press. 32 pages, 4.25" by 5.5". Publication Date: 12 February 1991. ISBN 0-926935-42-9.

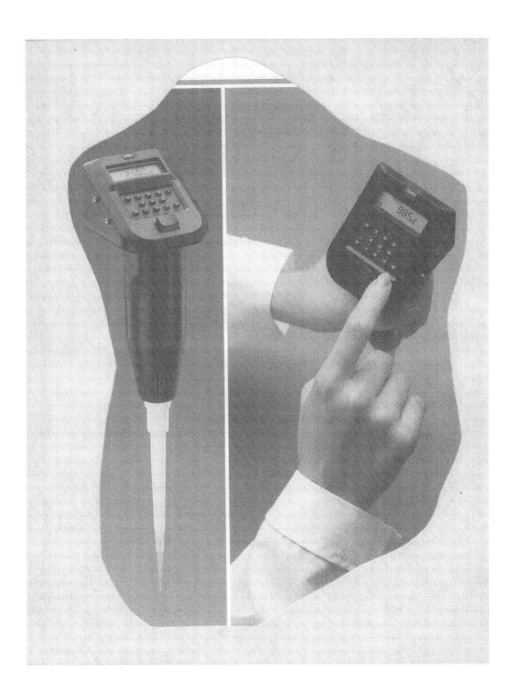

PLANET OF THE

What On

EA

Are We

THE LAST ACTS OF SAINT FUCK YOU by Bern Porter
Printed in the Autonomous Republic of Qazingulaza

Made in the USA
Charleston, SC
29 September 2010